Magic Ponies

Pony Camp

To Daisy-May, a challenge,

but always fun and warmhearted—SB

GROSSET & DUNLAP
Published by the Penguin Group
Penguin Group (USA) LLC, 375 Hudson Street, New York, New York 10014, USA

USA | Canada | UK | Ireland | Australia | New Zealand | India | South Africa | China

penguin.com
A Penguin Random House Company

Text copyright © 2009 by Sue Bentley. Illustrations copyright © 2009 by Angela Swan. Cover illustration © 2009 by Andrew Farley. First printed in Great Britain in 2009 by Penguin Books Ltd. First published in the United States in 2014 by Grosset & Dunlap, a division of Penguin Young Readers Group, 345 Hudson Street, New York, New York 10014. GROSSET & DUNLAP is a trademark of Penguin Group (USA) LLC. Printed in the U.S.A.

Library of Congress Cataloging-in-Publication Data is available.

ISBN 978-0-448-46787-0   10 9 8 7 6 5

Magic Ponies

Pony Camp

SUE BENTLEY

illustrated by Angela Swan

Grosset & Dunlap
An Imprint of Penguin Group (USA) LLC

Prologue

Comet folded his gold-feathered wings as he drifted down to land on Rainbow Mist Island. The grass was lush and velvety beneath his shining hooves. It felt good to be home.

But the magic pony's happiness faded as he thought of his twin sister. Destiny had been gone for so long. Surely she would have found her way back here by now.

He trotted hopefully up the slope toward a small forest. Comet's deep violet eyes scanned the trees for signs of movement. Maybe Destiny was staying there, away from the hot sun.

Sunlight poured down onto Comet's cream coat and flowing mane and tail, which glimmered like spun gold silk. Comet paused to drink from a spring that bubbled over shimmering, moss-covered rocks.

The nearby trees were covered in light-pink and violet leaves that rustled softly in the breeze. Suddenly the ground shook as thudding hooves approached. Was it another pony from Comet's Lightning Herd or one of the fierce dark horses? Comet tensed, ready to turn and flee, but then hesitated.

Perhaps it was his twin sister, hurrying to greet him!

"Destiny?"

An older horse with glowing dark eyes burst into the open. Its nostrils were flared and it was breathing hard.

"Blaze!" Comet greeted the leader of the Lightning Herd. "What's wrong? Is Destiny with you?"

Blaze reared up onto his back legs. "It was a dark horse, but the stone helped me outrun it!" As he grew calmer, his dark eyes softened. "I am glad to see you again, my young friend. But I am afraid that Destiny has not come back."

Disappointment flooded through Comet. "She must think she is still in trouble."

The Lightning Herd's Stone of Power
protected them from the dark horses
who wanted to steal their magic. It had
been lost while Comet and Destiny were
playing a game of cloud-racing. Comet
had found the stone again, but Destiny
had already left.

"You must find her and tell her it is
safe to return." Blaze struck the grass with
one shining front hoof and a fiery opal
appeared.

As Comet drew closer, the Stone
grew larger and multicolored rays of light
streamed out from it. An image formed
in the center. He saw a pony galloping
across green fields in a world far away.

Comet's eyes widened. "There she is!"

There was a flash of bright violet light
and a drift of rainbow mist that swirled

around the magic pony. Where the
cream-colored winged pony had stood
there was now a glossy dark-brown Fell
pony with a white star on his forehead.

"Go now. Use this disguise," Blaze
urged. "Bring Destiny back safely!"

"I will," Comet vowed.

He whinnied as he felt the power
building within him. The swirling
multicolored mist thickened as it drew
him in.

Chapter
ONE

Lindsey Heaven's heart thudded
uncomfortably as the car and horse trailer
turned in through the imposing stone
gates. Acres of open fields and woodland
stretched away on either side. Hamilton
Hall, a large stone building, was on a hill
in the distance.

A sign pointing the other way read
HAMILTON RIDING.

"Look at that view!" Mr. Heaven exclaimed as he headed toward the riding center. "I bet you're already imagining going for a ride on Allsorts."

"Mmm," Lindsey murmured vaguely, feeling another flutter of nerves.

Allsorts was Lindsey's pony. It had been her mom and dad's idea for her to come to pony camp. They thought she spent too much time alone and needed to meet more kids her own age. And they

weren't sure if they could afford to keep
Allsorts for much longer and wanted
Lindsey to enjoy camp with her own
pony.

"Ah, here we are." Mr. Heaven spotted
a number of small log cabins through the
trees.

"Lindsey is in number four," Mrs.
Heaven said. "There it is, over there. It'll
be fun to sleep in a cabin. They look really
cozy."

My bedroom's even cozier, Lindsey
thought, wishing she was there right now.

She took a deep breath as she
nervously imagined having to share a
room with other kids. She hoped they'd
be easy to get along with. She really did
want to try and make new friends.

They pulled up in front of the rows

of cabins and her dad got her suitcase out of the trunk. There were cars and horse trailers everywhere. Lindsey could see kids through open cabin doors, dumping their suitcases, calling out greetings, and choosing beds.

A slim woman with a blond ponytail seemed to be in charge. She smiled at Lindsey. "Hi! I'm Gina Morgan, chief instructor. Welcome to Hamilton Riding."

Lindsey smiled shyly. "Thank you," she said politely. "I'm Lindsey Heaven."

The woman checked her name off on a clipboard. "Go right in, Lindsey. Two of your cabinmates have already arrived. The other's been held up, but is on her way. You can start getting to know each other while your parents take your pony to the stable."

Lindsey swallowed hard. "You'll . . . you'll come and say good-bye before you leave, won't you?"

"Of course we will!" Mrs. Heaven patted her daughter's arm. "Off you go now. We'll see to Allsorts."

"Thanks, Mom. Tell him I'll come and give him a hug later."

Lindsey watched the car and horse trailer pulling away and then went into the cabin. Sunlight was pouring in through two large windows. Four beds were in the roomy cabin, one placed on either side of each window. Bright yellow curtains and checkered sheets made the room cheerful and welcoming.

Two girls had already claimed the beds nearest to the bathroom door. They were unpacking suitcases and folding clothes into chests of drawers.

One of them turned around. She was tall and pretty with shiny brown hair and fashionable-looking clothes. She seemed about eleven years old. "I'm Natasha Smart, but I only speak to people if they call me Tash," she said curtly.

"Um . . . Hi, Tash. I'm Lindsey, but everyone calls me Lins," Lindsey replied, a bit thrown by Natasha's abruptness.

Tash just nodded toward the other girl. "That's Shawna, and just so you know, she's *my* best friend."

Lindsey's heart sank. It was obvious Tash didn't care about making friends like she did. This was turning out to be just like school. She wandered sadly over to one of the spare beds.

"This place is cool, isn't it?" Shawna said. Freckles dotted her pale skin and she wore her long red hair in a braid.

"Um . . . yeah, it seems really nice—" Lindsey began, in an effort to be friendly to the other older girl. But then she realized that Shawna was talking to Tash.

"Duh!" Tash mocked. "What a dummy!"

The two girls giggled and rolled their eyes.

Lindsey felt herself blushing and wished she could sink into the floor. Opening her suitcase, she tried to ignore the other girls as she began putting her clothes in her dresser.

"So, which pony camps have you been to?" Shawna called out. "Hey! You listening?"

Lindsey realized that she was being spoken to this time. "I haven't been to camp before. This is my first one."

"Oh great!" Tash snorted. "We're stuck with a camp newbie! Are you any good at riding?"

Lindsey's cheeks were practically burning. She knew she must be as red as a beet. "I'm . . . um, okay, I think," she said modestly. The riding-school owner said she was actually pretty good, but Lindsey didn't like to boast.

"Well, you'd better be! We don't want any lame ducks losing us team points!" Tash retorted.

Shawna laughed and chucked her

pillow at Tash. "I'm done unpacking. Let's go explore!"

Linking arms, the friends wandered out together.

"See you later," Lindsey called, but neither of the other girls answered. The cabin door slammed shut in her face.

She plonked herself down onto her bed. How was she going to get through the next week with those two? Shawna was tolerable, but Tash was an absolute nightmare. Lindsey just hoped that the final girl, who had yet to arrive, would be nicer than they were.

She was still sitting there when her mom and dad came to say good-bye. "Everything's taken care of. Allsorts is in his stall, and you can go and see him whenever you'd like," her mom told her.

Her dad ruffled her short brown hair.
"So we're going to go now. See you next
week. Have a wonderful time. And we'll
call you in the morning."

There was a horrible sinking feeling
in Lindsey's tummy, and she only just
managed to stop herself from begging

them to take her home with them. Instead she gave them a big hug and said her good-byes. Outside the cabin, she waved until their car was out of sight.

Sighing heavily, she wondered what to do next. Finally, she decided to go and find the stables. There was a path through the woods and some buildings in the distance. She set off through the trees.

Lindsey was only just out of sight of the cabin when she reached a clearing. There was a sudden bright flash and a patch of glittering multicolored mist appeared and filled the whole area in front of her. She noticed rainbow droplets twinkling on her bare arms.

"Oh!" Lindsey scrunched her face, trying to see through the strange mist.

As it slowly cleared, she spotted a

pretty dark-brown Fell pony, with a white star on its forehead, walking toward her. "Can you help me, please?" it asked in a velvety whinny.

Chapter
TWO

Lindsey's eyes widened as she stared at
the pretty pony in complete astonishment.

She didn't know what a pony was doing
loose in the woods, but she did know that
it couldn't possibly have talked to her! She
shook her head slowly, thinking that she
must be imagining things.

She walked toward the pony, with her
hands at her sides so she wouldn't alarm it.

"Hello, there," she said, in a soft, encouraging voice. "Aren't you gorgeous? How did you manage to escape? I bet everyone's looking for you. I'd better find the stables and take you back there."

The pony's ears twitched and it lifted its head proudly. "I did not escape from anywhere. I have just arrived here from Rainbow Mist Island."

Lindsey stopped in her tracks. "Y-you really c-can talk?" she stuttered. "Or is this some kind of trick?"

She looked around nervously, expecting to see Tash hiding behind a tree, ready to jump out and make fun of her. It seemed like the kind of thing she might do. But there was no one in sight.

She turned back to the pony, frowning in puzzlement. For the first time, she

noticed that it had unusually deep violet eyes.

"I am Comet of the Lightning Herd. What is your name?" it neighed politely.

Lindsey blinked, finally having to accept that something totally amazing was happening. "I'm . . . I'm Lindsey Heaven, but everyone calls me Lins. I'm here at pony camp."

Comet dipped his head in a formal

bow and his dark brown mane fell forward. "I am honored to meet you, Lins."

Lindsey hesitated. Should she curtsy or something? She settled for awkwardly leaning forward. "Um . . . me too." The shock started to wear off, and her curiosity took over. "No offense, but why did you come here?"

Comet snorted and twitched his tail. "I am looking for my twin sister who is lost and in hiding. She is called Destiny."

Lindsey looked around for another magic pony, but this part of the woods was empty except for her and Comet. "But why is Destiny in hiding? Is someone after her?" she asked.

Comet's neck drooped a little with sadness. "We were playing cloud-racing in the night sky, when Destiny accidentally lost the Stone of Power. The stone protects the Lightning Herd from the dark horses who want to steal our magic. I found it again, but Destiny had already left. Now she is far away from the stone's protection and in danger of being found by the dark horses."

Lindsey listened hard. It all sounded so magical and strange. But one thing he said was bothering her. "You and Destiny were cloud-racing? In the sky? But how—"

"Please stay there," Comet whinnied, backing away.

Lindsey felt a warm prickling sensation, like pins and needles flowing through her fingers right to the tips. Violet sparkles bloomed in Comet's dark-brown coat and a light rainbow mist whirled around him. The pretty Fell pony disappeared and in his place stood a large, regal cream-colored pony, with a flowing golden mane and tail. Springing from his shoulders were magnificent, gleaming gold-feathered wings.

Lindsey gasped. Nothing could have prepared her for such a beautiful sight. She was speechless with wonder.

"Comet?" she breathed, when she could finally speak.

"Yes, it is still me, Lins. There is nothing to fear," Comet said in a deep, musical neigh. There was a final flash and a swirl of glittering mist, and Comet reappeared as a pretty dark-brown pony with a white star on his forehead.

"Wow! That's a brilliant disguise. Can Destiny do that, too?"

Comet nodded. "But no disguise will save her if our enemies discover her," he snorted gravely. "I must look for her. Will you help me?"

Lindsey felt a flicker of doubt. The dark horses sounded fierce and dangerous. What

would a nervous scaredy-cat like her be able
to do against them? But then the magic
pony came right up to her. Leaning forward,
he pushed his satiny nose into her hand.

Lindsey's heart melted as she felt
Comet huffing warm breath onto her
fingers. "Of course I will—we'll search
for Destiny together."

"Thank you, Lins."

"Just wait until you meet Tash and Shawna. That'll show them who's . . ."

Comet pulled back his ears. "No! I am sorry, Lins. You can tell no one about me or what I have told you!"

Lindsey was confused. It was going to be pretty hard to keep Comet a secret. A loose pony that didn't belong to anyone was bound to attract attention. She told Comet this.

"You must promise," the magic pony insisted. "All will be well, Lins."

As Lindsey looked into his intelligent eyes, she felt a warm, happy glow spread through her and realized that she trusted him completely. "Well—okay, then," she agreed, smiling. "Cross my heart."

"Thank you, Lins."

"I'll try to slip away and meet you later, once I find out how things work here," she told him. "This place is huge. There are acres of fields and woods with lakes where Destiny could be hiding."

Suddenly a loud voice called out, "What*ever* are you doing, talking to yourself? You're a bit old to have an imaginary friend, aren't you?"

Lindsey looked up to see Tash coming toward her. She took a deep breath. How was she going to explain about Comet?

"Um . . . I was just—" she began.

"Save it for someone who's interested," Tash interrupted rudely. "I'm missing out on the yummy welcome lunch because I was sent to find you! We're in the Hay Net restaurant. So, hurry up, okay?" She whirled around and jogged away in the

direction of a large building, just visible
through the trees.

"Yeah, okay. I'll be . . . um, right
there!" Lindsey called after her.

She was confused. Why hadn't Tash
said something about the dark-brown
Fell pony standing there as large as life? It
was almost as if she hadn't noticed him.
Lindsey didn't get it.

When she turned back to Comet, she
saw that his large violet eyes were glowing
with amusement. "I used my magic so that

only you will be able to see and hear me," he explained.

"You can make yourself invisible? Oh, wow! That makes things a lot easier!" Lindsey exclaimed. Reaching out she scratched gently at the white star between Comet's eyes. She smiled as he lowered his head in enjoyment.

Her lonely stay at pony camp with two awful cabinmates looked like it was going to be a lot more fun now that she had a magic pony for a special friend!

Chapter THREE

Tash had been right about one thing.
The food in the Hay Net was delicious.
Lindsey polished off tons of sandwiches
and cupcakes, and a huge slice of yummy
chocolate cake.

Everyone around her was chatting and
laughing. Lots of them seemed to know
each other from previous pony camps. No
one paid Lindsey much attention, but she

didn't mind so much now. She was used to it, and, anyway, she couldn't wait to go back to the woods to see Comet, even if it was just to prove to herself that she hadn't dreamed the whole thing.

She stood up and began weaving her way through the tables.

"Off to meet up with your imaginary friend again?" Tash called after her.

Lindsey half-turned, blushing again. She hated being teased, especially as she could never think of a clever reply.

"I'm going to . . . finish unpacking,"
she murmured, looking down at the floor.
*Actually I'm going to meet my magic pony
friend. But you wouldn't believe me, even if I
told you. Which I'm never going to!*

"Unpacking. Wow! That's so exciting!"
Tash smirked, slapping Shawna on the
back.

Unfortunately for Shawna, she had a
big mouthful of the chocolate cake and
Lindsey almost laughed out loud as she
spluttered half of it back onto the table.

Lindsey soon forgot about Tash and
Shawna as she eagerly hurried through the
woods. She soon reached the place where
Comet had appeared.

"Comet!" she whispered.

There was no answer.

She walked through the trees, looking

to the right and the left, and then retraced
her steps to look again. But the dark-
brown Fell pony wasn't there. Lindsey's
spirits fell. Maybe Comet had changed
his mind about being her friend and had
found someone else to help him search
for Destiny.

She decided to come back later just in
case Comet had returned. She desperately
hoped so. Her shoulders slumped a little
in disappointment at not seeing her
special friend as she walked back to the
cabin.

Lindsey emerged from the trees to see
a girl standing outside her cabin. The girl
bent down to pick up her suitcase, and
the handle came off in her hand.

Thump! There was a loud clatter
as the suitcase fell to the ground. It

burst open and the contents spilled out.

"Oh no!" the girl groaned loudly.
"First our car breaks down and we have
to wait about a hundred years for the tow
truck. And now my useless suitcase dies on
me!"

Lindsey hurried toward her. "Let me
help you," she offered, already scrambling
around on the floor to gather up scattered
socks, T-shirts, and shorts.

"Oh, thanks. I didn't know anyone was there." Smiling, the girl tucked a strand of light-brown hair behind one ear. She had a round face and lively brown eyes. "I'm Penny. Penny Cookson."

"Hi, Penny. I'm Lindsey. You must be our fourth cabinmate."

"I am!" Penny declared. "And I'm so hungry I could eat a grizzly bear squashed between two mattresses. I bet I've missed lunch, too, haven't I?"

Lindsey nodded, grinning, as she opened the door and dumped an armful of stuff onto the empty bed. "Yeah, 'fraid so. It was pretty good, too, especially the cake. We could go and see if there's anything left. I can show you where the Hay Net is. That's the restaurant, where we have all our meals."

"That would be great! I just have to put these out first." Opening a zip-up bag, Penny took out a collection of toy ponies and lined them up on top of her bedside chest.

"Wow! Those are really cute!" Lindsey admired the tiny pretty faces, bright glass eyes, and silky manes and tails. "They're so lifelike. Do they have names?"

"You bet! This one's Spot, and that's Fudge, and this one's my favorite, Petal the Palomino . . ." Penny had just finished reeling off the names of all the tiny horses when Tash and Shawna came in.

Tash took one look at the messy heap of clothes and other stuff. "You'd better clean that up, right now!" she said, bossily. "We'll lose team points for leaving the cabin in a mess."

Lindsey felt bad for the new girl.
She'd hardly set foot in the place and Tash
was already being mean to her. "It wasn't
Penny's fault!" She forgot to be shy as she
defended the new girl. "Her suitcase br—"

Tash glared at her. "What's it got to do
with you?"

Penny gently put a hand on Lindsey's
arm. "Thanks, but it's okay," she said softly,
before turning to Tash. "So where's your
badge?"

"Huh? What badge?" Tash looked
puzzled.

"The one that says, *I'm in charge!*"
Penny quipped.

Tash looked taken aback for a
moment. "I was only saying!" she
countered and then her eyes gleamed
spitefully. "What sort of a name's Penny,

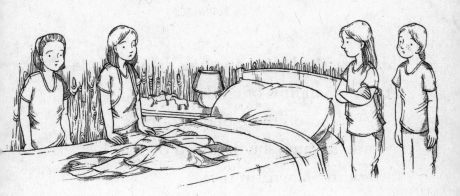

anyway? Who'd want to be called after a
measly cheap brown coin?"

"That's a good one, Tash!" Shawna
tittered.

"Tash?" Penny said, her mouth
twitching. "You should talk! You're named
after a bit of fuzz under a man's nose!"

"I am not!" Tash spluttered, going red.
"Tash is short for Natasha!"

"Ooh, I do beg your pardon!" Penny
mocked, in a stuffy, old-fashioned voice.
"Well, I'd love to chat, but I've got some
cleaning up to do." Ignoring Tash and

Shawna, she began opening drawers and
stuffing handfuls of clothes inside.

Tash stood there openmouthed.
Moments later, she flounced over to her
bed with Shawna in tow.

Lindsey bit back a grin as she looked
at Penny in admiration. She didn't want
to hope too much that she'd met a real
friend but, either way, Penny was a whole
lot nicer than either Tash or Shawna!

As her cabinmates got ready for bed,
Lindsey fidgeted impatiently. After visiting
Allsorts in the stable that evening to make
sure the black-and-white pony was settled
in, she'd cut back through the woods,
looking for Comet. But there was still
no sign of the magic pony. She lay there

trying to think of an excuse to go back outside again, but nothing came to mind.

Tash and Shawna were lying on their beds in their pajamas, chatting and flipping through pony magazines, and Penny was in the bathroom. Lindsey sighed. It looked as if she was going to have to wait until the other girls were asleep before she could slip out.

Only half concentrating, she reached for the book on the top of her bedside chest. Her fingers brushed lightly against a tiny toy pony.

Lindsey frowned. Weird. What was one of Penny's toys doing near her bed?

She looked more closely at the tiny pony, which was dark brown with a white star on its forehead and big deep violet eyes. It looked a lot like . . .

The toy pony suddenly shook itself and its ears twitched forward.

"Comet?" Lindsey gasped. "Is it really you? What are you doing here?"

"I was waiting for you to come and meet me in the woods, and I saw how many people there are at pony camp," he told her in tiny soft neigh that matched his new size. "I thought it might be difficult for you to sneak out without being seen. So this seemed like a better way for us to be together."

"And it's much more fun!" Lindsey whispered delightedly. She felt a surge of affection for her magical friend. He was so thoughtful. "This is so cool! Now you can sleep on my bed and be warm and cozy if it rains. And I can take you everywhere with me in my bag. You can even ride Allsorts with me."

Comet whinnied with pleasure. "I
would like that. And we can look for
Destiny at the same time."

"You've thought of everything!"
Lindsey said. Comet was full of surprises.
She wondered what else her magic friend
could do.

Reaching out, she gently picked
him up and then sat with him in her lap.
Comet was pretty as a dark-brown Fell

pony and magnificent as his beautiful golden-winged self—but right now he was the cutest, most adorable toy pony imaginable.

She was so busy stroking his tiny ears and petal-soft coat and admiring his tiny perfect hooves that she didn't notice Tash watching her with raised eyebrows.

Suddenly Tash bounded across the room. "What are you doing with Penny's toy pony? I bet you didn't ask her if you could have it."

Before Lindsey could stop her she grabbed Comet roughly. The tiny pony gave a whinny of dismay as Tash walked off with him.

Chapter FOUR

Lindsey froze, waiting for Tash to notice that Comet was real. But, just like in the woods, when Tash hadn't been able to see Comet at all, she now seemed only to be able to see him as a normal toy.

Lindsey realized that her new friend's secret was still safe. But she didn't know whether his magic would protect him from being hurt. Tash was holding him so tightly he could hardly breathe. She had to get him back.

Leaping off the bed, Lindsey launched herself across the room. "Comet's not Penny's. He's mine! Give him back!" she demanded.

"Make me!" Tash crowed, holding him in the air.

Lindsey tried to jump up and grab Comet, but Tash was taller than she was and she couldn't reach.

Tash tossed the toy toward Shawna. "Here! Catch!"

Lindsey heard Comet give a tiny frightened neigh as Shawna just managed to grab him by one leg.

"Stop it! You'll hurt him!" As she ran toward her, Shawna laughed and tossed Comet back to Tash.

"Oops!" Tash fumbled her catch and Comet was launched right up into the air.

Lindsey backed up, positioning herself to catch him as he plummeted downwards. *Yes! Got him!* Comet was safe, but as she turned, clutching him tightly, she banged heavily into a chair and twisted her ankle.

"Ow!" Tears of pain stung her eyes, but she swallowed hard, determined not to cry in front of the older girls. Holding Comet close, she hobbled over to her bed and sat down. "Are you okay?" she whispered, stroking him very gently.

Comet's tiny eyes glittered like amethysts. "I am not hurt, thanks to you. You were brave to save me from those two mean girls."

"I wasn't, really. I just couldn't bear

anything to happen to you," Lindsey said.
Now that the excitement was over, her
ankle began throbbing painfully and she
bit her lip.

"You have hurt yourself. Let me help,"
Comet neighed.

Lindsey felt a tingling sensation
flowing to the very tips of her fingers

as miniature violet sparks glowed in the tiny pony's coat and a glittering rainbow mist full of tiny multicolored stars swirled around her ankle. Gradually the colored mist sank into her pajama leg and then disappeared, as did every last one of the tiny violet sparks.

"Oh! My ankle feels fine now. Thanks, Comet," Lindsey said. She swung her legs up and lay back against her pillows, still holding him close.

"Honestly! Some people can't take a joke," Tash scoffed. Lindsey refused to even meet her gaze. "Collecting stupid toy ponies is pathetic anyway."

The bathroom door opened. Penny came out and stood in the cabin with her hands on her hips. "Did I hear someone say that collecting toy ponies is pathetic?"

she asked, looking pointedly toward Tash.

Tash's expression changed. "Um . . . no! It's great. I love toy ponies," Tash said, hurriedly jumping into bed.

Penny came and got into bed too. "Night, Lindsey," she said, switching off her bedside lamp.

"Night, Penny. Night, Comet," Lindsey whispered happily, cradling him close as she snuggled up with him under the covers.

Over breakfast in the Hay Net the following morning, Penny was trying to cheer up Lindsey. Her mom and dad had just called with bad news about Allsorts: They were going to have to sell him as soon as possible. Lindsey was feeling incredibly sad. It seemed like things were

going from bad to worse! She wondered
if Comet would come home to live with
her—perhaps she would ask him later on.

"It would be best-turned-out pony
first," Penny joked. "I'm terrible at
cleaning tack. It always looks worse than it
did before I started."

Lindsey smiled gratefully, as she
chewed on a bit of toast. She had one
hand on Comet, who sat on her lap, out
of sight beneath the table. "Don't worry,

I'll help you. I'm a total whizz with a damp sponge and a tin of saddle soap!"

Penny laughed. "You're on!"

A cheerful buzz of voices and laughter filled the big, bright room. The delicious smell of bacon cooking wafted from the self-service counter. Tash and Shawna were sitting at a nearby table. Looking over at Lindsey and Penny, they nudged each other and whispered. Lindsey just knew they were talking about Allsorts.

"Those two are awful!" Penny said, shaking her head.

"I know. I try to ignore them," Lindsey said, reaching down to stroke Comet's tiny silky mane.

"I am going to become normal size now, Lins. I will see you outside later," Comet whickered softly and disappeared in a little burst of invisible violet sparkles.

Lindsey and Penny finished eating and began strolling toward the tack room together. "Should we go and say hello to our ponies first?" Lindsey suggested.

"You bet. I can't wait to ride Chance," Penny told her. "Wait until you see her. She's so pretty, and she does anything I ask her."

Penny's blue-roan mare was in the stall opposite where Allsorts stood with his head hanging over his door. Lindsey gave him a hug. "Hello, girl, how do you like your stable?"

Penny was giving Chance a peppermint. The pony had large kind eyes and a neat head with a slightly dished nose.

"What a lovely pony. Have you had her?"

"About a year or so. I'm looking for a
sharer for her," Penny said. She kissed her
pony's soft muzzle. "How about you?" she
asked.

But before Lindsey could answer,
Tash's mocking tones filled the stable.
"Ugh. Check out Penny, kissing her
horse—imagine all the germs she has!
Gross."

"Well, I'd rather kiss Chance than

kiss you any day, Natasha," Penny replied stressing Tash's full name that she hated so much.

Tash paused in the doorway and turned. She narrowed her eyes and gave Penny a really dirty look before pressing her lips together and stomping away.

Lindsey felt a prickle of unease. "You shouldn't provoke, Penny," she warned.

"What's she going to do—nag me to death?" Penny said, laughing.

Lindsey grinned and forgot all about Tash as she and Penny continued strolling to the tack room. "So, about cleaning tack," she started explaining. "First we have to take it all apart . . ."

Chapter
FIVE

At first, Lindsey found it strange to have Comet beside her when no one else could see the magic pony. Once or twice, during the activities, she almost turned to talk to him, but managed to catch herself just in time.

It was late in the afternoon before everyone was given a couple of hours of free time to do what they liked. Lindsey

seized on it eagerly. It was her first chance
to help Comet search for Destiny.

But Penny had other ideas. "I'll just
get a drink, then we can go out for a ride.
Okay?" she enthused.

"Um . . . okay," Lindsey murmured,
taken by surprise. She stared after Penny as
the other girl disappeared into the stable
kitchen.

She felt torn. If she went riding with
Penny and Chance, she wouldn't be able
to help Comet. But she'd already promised
they could go and look for Destiny.

She had seconds to decide what to do
before Penny emerged.

"Follow me, Comet." On impulse,
Lindsey mounted Allsorts and quickly
rode off, with Comet following closely
behind.

But as she glanced over her shoulder, she saw Penny standing in the doorway. "Hey! Lins! Wait up!" she cried, looking hurt and puzzled.

"I'm sorry! I won't be long." Lindsey felt bad. But she had no choice except to keep on going, if she wanted to avoid awkward questions. She would just have to try to make things up to Penny later and hope Penny understood.

Lindsey pointed Allsorts toward the bridle path that led through the woods. Comet pounded along beside them, his shining hooves making no sound. He whinnied at Allsorts and the little pony nickered back. Lindsey smiled as the two ponies made friends.

"I hope you haven't been too bored just hanging around all day," she said to Comet.

"It has been very interesting," he neighed. "I liked it when Penny waved her arms about and did a little dance."

"That was when she got the top grade for best-turned-out pony," she answered Comet. "The instructor said Penny's tack was practically glowing and she needed sunglasses to look at it!"

Comet swished his tail. "It was kind of you to help her with her tack. I like Penny. She seems like a nice girl."

"Yeah, she is. I wish I was as funny and confident as she is. Nothing fazes her." *Not like me*, she thought, feeling another pang of guilt at having ridden off and left Penny standing there. "Anyway, let's go looking for Destiny!" Lindsey said, changing the subject. She felt better at the thought of spending some time helping Comet at last.

Comet tossed his head and pawed at the ground with one front hoof. As he leaped forward, Lindsey urged on Allsorts. The little black-and-white pony snorted and quickened his pace.

The ponies galloped along side by side, Comet matching his longer stride to Allsorts's, and Lindsey felt happiness glow through her as they sped along. Sunshine filtered down through the trees, casting spots of golden light onto them.

They wove along the bridle paths, now and then passing other ponies and riders who waved and smiled. Slowing to a walk, Comet's keen eyes continually searched for signs of his lost twin.

At one point during their ride, they spotted a donkey and three ponies in a small paddock beside a cottage. Comet trotted up to them excitedly, his ears pricking. But none of the ponies was Destiny.

As Lindsey reached Comet she saw that his violet eyes had lost a little of their glow and his head was drooping slightly with disappointment. *He must be missing Destiny badly.* Her heart moved with sympathy for her friend.

"We'll find her, don't worry," she reassured him. "This camp is huge. There're

tons of places where Destiny could be
hiding. She might even have come past here
recently."

"I would have known if she had," Comet
neighed. "She would have left a trail."

"A trail? What would it look like?"

"It would be a line of softly glowing
hoofprints. But most humans would not be
able to see it."

Lindsey was fascinated. "Will I be able to
see it?"

Comet nodded. "Yes. If you are riding me or we are very close."

"Cool! That should make it easier to find her. Maybe, when you do, you could both come and live with me," she said hopefully. "I'll be going home from camp in a few days. You'll like it where I live."

"I am afraid that is not possible," Comet neighed. "I must take Destiny back to our family on Rainbow Mist Island. I hope you understand, Lins."

Lindsey nodded mutely as she forced herself to accept that Comet would not be staying forever. But she didn't want to think about that. He was here now, and she wanted to enjoy every single moment with him.

"Shall we go on searching?" she said.

"What about over there? That looks

like a farm up on that hill."

Comet nodded and glanced around with renewed interest as they set off again. After a long, steep ride, they crested the hill. But they had no luck with the farm and its outbuildings. They paused to look down into the valley before they went on.

Allsorts was panting, and his sides were heaving. Lindsey decided she'd better take the little black-and-white pony back.

"He's willing to go on, but I've ridden him quite hard. I think he needs a drink and then to rest and cool down," she reasoned.

Comet neighed agreement. "Allsorts is a fine pony. He has done well. But if you were to ride me, we would be able to cover more ground and search for longer."

Lindsey realized that he was right, but

it was always going to be difficult to slip away by herself without someone noticing and asking awkward questions. "I think there's a movie night sometime soon. Everyone will be there. That would be a good time to sneak out to meet you."

"Thank you, Lins."

Lindsey smiled at him, feeling like the luckiest girl in the world. She was really looking forward to riding her very own magic pony friend.

Chapter
SIX

Lindsey left Comet nibbling the
sweet grass on the hillside. As soon as she
had given Allsorts a drink and rubbed
him down, she went looking for Penny.
She found her sitting in the living room,
flipping through a magazine and looking a
bit bored.

Lindsey went over to her. "Hi, what
are you doing?" she asked quietly. She

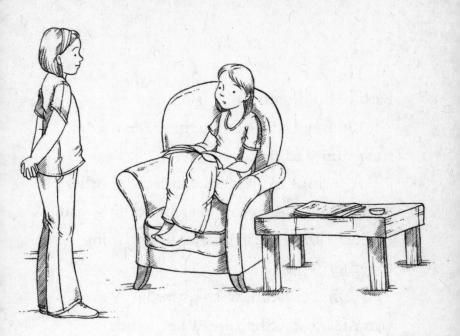

really hoped Penny wasn't too mad at her
for riding off earlier.

Penny looked up. "Oh, hi. I came here
for a bit of peace. Tash, Shawna, and a
couple of other girls are having a picnic
outside the cabin."

"Didn't you want to join them for the
picnic?"

Penny rolled her eyes. "With Tash
bossing everyone about? I'd rather sit in a

bath of cold oatmeal!"

Lindsey burst out laughing. Penny said such funny things.

A serious expression crossed the other girl's face. "Didn't you hear me calling you earlier? I thought we were going riding together?"

"Oh, I . . . um, wasn't sure if you meant it!" She spread her hands apologetically. "I'm so sorry. I messed up."

Penny's face cleared and she smiled. "Don't worry about it. I ended up exploring around the big lake. It was great to give Chance a good long ride. Maybe we can go riding in the woods together another time?"

"Definitely," Lindsey said, relieved. Thank goodness Penny had accepted her explanation. She would have hated to

upset her, especially now it seemed they
really were becoming friends, but at the
same time she had to keep her promise to
Comet.

It rained heavily overnight and it
was still raining the following morning.
There were puddles everywhere and the
ground squelched beneath Lindsey's riding
boots as she made her way to the stable
yard.

Inside, Lindsey reached for the body
brush from the grooming kit by Allsorts's
stall and began working on his black-and-
white coat with long, firm strokes.

The stable gradually filled up with
other kids. Sounds of laughter, pony
noises, and rustling hay filled the air.
Not long after, Penny came in to groom

Chance, and the two girls chatted as they worked. Soon their ponies' coats were gleaming.

Lindsey admired Chance's unusual blue-roan coat. "She's so gorgeous. Your sharer is going be a lucky rider."

Penny nodded. "It might be a bit difficult to find one. We're moving to Blakestone soon after I get back from camp."

"Blakestone! But that's only a few miles away from where I live!" Lindsey said delightedly.

Before Penny could reply, Gina Morgan walked in. "Listen up, everyone. We'll be doing stable management today and training work in the yard tomorrow," she announced. "Cross-country and team games will take place when the weather's better. Sorry, but we'll be mostly indoors today, guys."

There were a few groans of disappointment at not being able to go out riding on the ponies.

Lindsey had been looking forward to riding Allsorts, with Comet galloping alongside them again as they both kept an eye out for Destiny. She hoped Comet had found somewhere dry to shelter until this awful weather broke.

"Greetings, Lins," his soft neigh sounded close to her and she felt his breath ruffle her hair.

"Oh!" She almost jumped out of her skin.

Lindsey bit back a grin as she turned and saw Comet's head hanging over the door of an empty stall behind her. His deep violet eyes were glinting cheekily. She wished she could give her invisible magic pony a hug, but she didn't want to risk it with so many people in the stable.

Gina was now talking about skips, brushes, and hay forks. "It's good practice to get used to putting things away. Leaving things lying around can cause accidents to you and your pony . . ."

"No one can tell me anything about

stable management," Tash boasted. She
looked sideways at Lindsey. "You learn a
lot from looking after your own pony. I've
been taking care of Jewel ever since Dad
bought him." Jewel was her showy black
thoroughbred gelding.

Lindsey tried to ignore Tash's
comment, but she knew the other girl was
referring to her losing Allsorts soon. She
chewed at her bottom lip.

"Is something wrong, Lins?" Comet
whinnied.

"It's Tash. She's such a pain. I've had
enough of her little digs at me!" she
whispered angrily.

Comet twitched his ears thoughtfully.

"Muck piles," Gina said. "Not very
glamorous maybe, but they're a fact of life
for pony lovers. They can easily spread out

of control, unless you're firm with them. Right?"

There was a ripple of agreement.

"The thing to do is to give some thought about building them up. It's not enough to tip your wheelbarrow and run away .You want a muck heap with a dip in the center, like a saucer, not heaped up in a soggy mess. So it's build and squash— jump up and down on it every day."

"Anyone knows that!" Tash commented to Shawna.

The instructor looked at her. "If you're such an expert, why don't you demonstrate for the rest of us? There's a wheelbarrow of soiled bedding over there."

"Sure!" Tash smiled confidently. She took hold of the handles and wheeled the light plastic wheelbarrow to the muck pile across the yard. Everyone watched as she pushed it up the steep ramp.

Lindsey felt a familiar tingling feeling flow down her fingers as violet sparkles glinted in Comet's dark-brown coat, and a fine rainbow mist, invisible to everyone but Lindsey, swirled around Tash and the wheelbarrow. *What's he up to?* Lindsey wondered.

The rainbow mist dissolved into
glittery dust and disappeared. Suddenly
the wheelbarrow seemed to give a jaunty
little skip and tipped backward. The pile
of smelly hay teetered. And a huge mess of
hay and smelly poo fell, splattering all over
Tash.

Everyone fell about laughing.

"Oh, Comet. That was mean!" Lindsey
spluttered. "But she deserved it!"

Penny was helpless with laughter.

"Oh dear," the instructor said, her lips
twitching. "Are you all right, Tash?"

"No! This is my best designer top!"
Tash said through gritted teeth. She
stalked back out to the yard and stood
picking strands of smelly hay off her
clothes.

"Phew! Anyone got a spare

clothespin?" Penny said, holding her nose.

"Oh, shut up!" Tash fumed, looking at her angrily. "You think you're so clever, don't you, Penny Cookson? Well, we'll see who has the last laugh!"

"Uh-oh," Lindsey whispered worriedly to Comet. "I don't like the sound of that."

Chapter SEVEN

Despite Lindsey's fears, nothing else happened between Tash and Penny. In fact, they appeared to be ignoring each other. *Which is probably for the best*, she thought.

By the following afternoon, the rain had stopped and the yard had dried out a bit. Lindsey watched as Allsorts trotted in a circle while Gina held him on a lunge rein.

"Show Allsorts what you want him to do, okay? That's how you get a pony to adjust his stride. Now you try," the instructor handed her the rein.

Lindsey took it and did as she'd been shown. Allsorts obligingly lengthened his stride and cantered around in a wider circle.

"That's it. Well done," Gina praised.

Lindsey smiled, proud of the way Allsorts held himself as she put him through his paces. She would miss the little pony very much.

The rest of the day passed quickly. And just before dinner, everyone went back to their cabins to change out of their riding kit.

Lindsey was taking her muddy boots off when, from inside their cabin, Penny gave a yell. "My favorite toy pony! Petal the Palomino. She's gone!"

"Maybe you put her away somewhere," Lindsey suggested.

"No, I didn't. Petal was right here on my bedside chest with all the others this morning!" Penny opened drawers and looked under the bed.

Lindsey and Penny practically turned the cabin upside down, but there was no sign of the tiny palomino pony.

By now, Penny was close to tears. "Someone took her. And I know who! Tash!"

Lindsey suspected that Penny might be right. She'd been afraid of something like this happening. "Let's go and tell Gina Morgan," she suggested.

Penny swallowed, crestfallen. "What's the point? We don't have any proof. Besides, I've never been a tattletale, and I'm not starting now."

"You could ask Tash and see what she says. Maybe she'll give Petal back if she sees how upset you are," Lindsey suggested.

"I wouldn't hold your breath," Penny

said bleakly. "She can't stand me. And I feel the same way about her." She took a big breath and wiped her eyes. "Well—I'm not going to let her see me cry. Would you come with me to the movie room? It's *National Treasure*—one of my favorites. And it's all about a racehorse, so I'm sure it'll cheer me up in the meantime."

Lindsey's heart sank. She'd promised to meet Comet, but how could she leave Penny now when she was upset and needed her—especially after riding off the other day? She racked her brain trying to think of a solution as she walked toward the main building with Penny.

The movie was really good, but Lindsey couldn't concentrate. All she could think of was Comet waiting for her in the woods.

After a while, she leaned over to whisper in Penny's ear. "I have headache, and I . . . um, feel a bit sick. I think I'll go back to the cabin."

"Poor you. I'll come and take care of you," Penny said at once.

"Don't worry," Lindsey whispered hastily. "Thanks, but I'll be fine. I'll probably just go to sleep. You stay and watch the movie. I'll see you later."

"Well, okay then. If you're sure," Penny said.

Lindsey nodded and slipped outside, leaving Penny engrossed in the movie. She set off in the direction of the woods and found Comet waiting patiently. He whinnied softly and took a step toward her.

"Hi, Comet." She reached out to stroke his silky dark-brown neck. "Sorry I'm late. I only just managed to get away."

"You are here now. Thank you, Lins," Comet neighed, tossing his head. "Climb onto my back."

Excitement stirred inside Lindsey as she mounted Comet and took a firm grip on "Let's go!"

"Hold tight!" Comet snorted eagerly and sprang forward into a gallop.

Lindsey crouched low on his back,
moving in time to his strides, and
her breath caught in her throat with
excitement as they raced along. Comet
was thrilling to ride, so smooth and fast.
His magic seemed to swirl around them
as he flew along. His shining hooves
barely touched the grass.

Moonlight silvered the trees and the
woods were a map of shadows. It was
very quiet. With no one else around
it could have been a bit creepy, but
Lindsey felt perfectly safe with Comet.

They left the woods and flashed
across fields, soaring up and down hills
and valleys with dizzying speed, looking
for Destiny. But they saw no signs of
any ponies.

"Let's try over there." Lindsey

pointed to Hamilton Hall, the stately stone house that she'd seen on the hill when her parents first drove her to pony camp.

After exploring the large gardens and grounds of Hamilton Hall, Comet headed for the lake. His hooves made no sound as they crossed a stone bridge. He paused and bent his head to the moonlit water that was as smooth as a deep-blue mirror. Ripples spread outwards as he drank.

Lindsey looked around her. The ghostly cry of an owl echoed in the still air. She felt as if there was no one else in the world except her and Comet. And she knew she would remember this special night for as long as she lived.

"We'd better go back soon," Lindsey said regretfully. She could happily have

ridden Comet for the entire night, but the
movie would soon be over. When Shawna,
Tash, and Penny returned to the cabin,
they were bound to notice if she wasn't in
bed.

Comet nodded. Pricking up his
ears he headed across the fields and back
to the woods. But as he approached the
trees, Lindsey felt him stiffen. He stopped
and leaned down to stare at the grass.

Lindsey looked down too. In front of

them and stretching away into the distance
was a faint line of softly glowing violet
hoofprints.

"Destiny! She came this way!" Comet
whinnied excitedly.

Lindsey felt a pang. Did that mean that
he was going to leave, right now? "Do you
want me to get down, so you can go after
her?" she asked anxiously.

Comet shook his head. "No, Lins. This
trail is cold. But it proves Destiny was
here." He pricked his ears forward again
with fresh hope. "When she is very close
I will be able to hear her hoofbeats. And
then I may have to leave suddenly, without
saying good-bye."

"Oh." Lindsey didn't think she could
bear it if that happened. She knew that
she had to face up to the fact that Comet

could not stay forever, but she would never be ready to lose her magical friend.

Comet snuffled Destiny's trail for a moment longer, lingering over the faint scent. Lindsey was touched by how much he missed his twin sister. He must love her very much. She leaned forward to pat his neck.

Raising his head, Comet shook himself. "I will take you back," he snorted.

Flicking his tail, he moved up into a full gallop and, once again, his long strides ate up the ground. In no time at all, the fields and woods were behind them and the cabin came into view.

Lindsey dismounted at the edge of the wood. She put her arms around Comet's neck and laid her cheek against his warm neck. Comet blew out warm breath and nuzzled her shoulder very gently.

She moved away reluctantly. "Night, Comet. I'll see you tomorrow."

"Good night, Lins."

As she walked away, he melted into the trees.

When Lindsey reached the cabin, the door opened and Penny flew out. "Lins! I came back to see if you were okay, and you weren't here. Where have you been?"

"I felt . . . um, a bit better, so I . . . um, went out for some fresh air." Lindsey stumbled over the hasty explanation. It wasn't exactly a lie. She had gulped huge lungfuls of fresh air while out riding Comet.

"But you were gone for ages. I was

just about to go and tell Gina Morgan that
I couldn't find you!"

"Sorry," Lindsey murmured. "I just lost
track of time."

Penny smiled, looking relieved. "Oh,
well, you're back now. Let's go inside. We
have to get up early tomorrow. It's cross-
country, remember?"

"Oh, yes!" Lindsey was looking forward to it. Allsorts loved jumping. It would be fun to see how well the plucky little pony did over a whole course of fences.

Inside the cabin, Penny gathered up her toy ponies, and she and Lindsey had a game of making them gallop over humps in the covers.

"I wish I knew where Petal the Palomino is," Penny said, looking downcast. "She was so pretty. My grandma bought her for my last birthday. I hate to think she might have been thrown away and I'll never see her again."

"Petal will turn up, you'll see," Lindsey said, hoping it was true.

She still felt sure that Tash knew something about Penny's missing toy, but

she had denied all knowledge when Penny
had asked her. Even if she had something
to do with Petal's disappearance, Lindsey
knew Tash would never admit it.

"Phew!" Lindsey breathed, as she
dismounted in the yard the following
afternoon. She was hot and sticky and
couldn't wait to take off her body-
protector and riding hat.

Penny rode up on Chance. "That was
great. I love cross-country. Allsorts did
really well." She slid down and tethered
the blue-roan pony.

"Yes, he did, didn't he?" Lindsey
agreed proudly, sliding up the stirrups and
undoing the girth straps. "He even gave
Jewel a run for his money. Did you see
Tash scowling at us?"

"It was hard to tell. She's always scowling," Penny said.

They both laughed.

"I can't believe that tomorrow's our last day," Lindsey said.

She was surprised by how sad she felt at the thought of leaving and she knew it wasn't just about losing Allsorts soon. She and Penny had become really good friends. And what was going to happen to Comet? Lindsey couldn't bear to leave him behind, sad and lonely and still looking for his lost twin sister.

"I know. The week's flown by, hasn't it?" Penny said. She waved a hand in front of Lindsey's face. "Hello? Are you listening?"

"Oh, sorry," Lindsey said, smiling, as she lifted off the heavy saddle. "I was miles away."

They carried their saddles and bridles into the tack room and then returned to hose down the sweaty ponies.

"Actually, Lins, there's something I've been meaning to ask you." Penny grinned, swooshing water off Chance's rump with a cupped hand. "You know how I'm going to be moving to Blakestone? Well, I have a favor to ask . . ."

Chapter EIGHT

Lindsey didn't have a single moment to herself for the rest of the day. After lunch there were team games. A pony-relay, a sack race, and then a catch-the-train race. The sight of Penny struggling into a floppy old-fashioned hat and baggy red dress, before running up to Chance and leaping onto her back was just too much! Lindsey laughed until her ribs ached.

In the evening there was a team treasure hunt, followed by karaoke. Once again it was impossible for Lindsey to get away. She decided that she would have to wait until everyone was asleep before going to meet Comet.

She lay in bed staring into the semidarkness as Tash and Shawna chatted and giggled annoyingly. But soon, despite their noise, her eyes started to droop.

Lindsey woke hours later to twittering birdsong. "Oh no! It's almost light out!" she murmured. Throwing back the covers, she quickly checked to see if the other girls were asleep, and then tiptoed outside.

"Comet!" she whispered, as she entered the woods. "Are you there?"

He appeared immediately at the edge of the woods. Morning mist swirled

around his legs, and the white star on his forehead stood out against his dark-brown coat. Snorting affectionately, he trotted to meet her.

Lindsey felt a deep thrill of wonder and excitement when she saw him. She knew she'd never take being Comet's friend for granted. He was her special secret, never to be told to anyone else.

The magic pony whickered softly and leaned forward, so that she could put her arms around his neck. "I don't have long. The others will be waking up soon, but I just had to see you. I've got some news!" she told him.

As she stood back, Comet blinked. "Has something happened?"

"Yes!" Lindsey exclaimed, bursting with excitement. "It's Penny. She asked me if I wanted to share her pony, Chance. I said I'd love to. She's moving close to me, so I'll be able to see her every day. We'll both look after Chance and take turns riding her. Isn't that amazing?"

Comet nuzzled her affectionately. "Yes. It is wonderful news."

But there was also something else Lindsey needed to tell Comet. She wasn't looking forward to it, but she couldn't put it off any longer. "After the prize-giving for most-improved rider, everyone will be leaving pony camp to go back home. I would love it so much if you would come back and live with me. But . . . but I don't think you can, can you?" she asked sadly.

Comet's violet eyes glistened, but he lifted his head proudly. "No. I must continue my search for Destiny. But do not worry about me, Lins—she is close."

But she knew she would worry. She couldn't help it. Sadness at the thought of leaving without him washed over her.

Part of her felt as if she had let Comet down in some way, although she knew she had done her best to keep her promise to him. She sighed; if only she could be certain that the lonely pony would be reunited with his lost sister. It would be awful never to know.

After giving Comet a final hug, Lindsey was about to slip quietly back into the cabin, when she had a sudden thought. "Penny's still really upset because her toy pony hasn't turned up. Petal the Palomino was her favorite. I'd love to find it for her. Do you think you could help me?"

"It would be my pleasure."

Almost at once, Lindsey felt a familiar prickling sensation flowing to her fingertips as violet sparkles twinkled in Comet's mane and tail and he blew out a big breath that turned into a glittering rainbow mist. As she stared at the mist, a picture formed of Tash's shoulder bag, sitting in the closet. Tucked away in the toe of a sock, right in the bottom, was a tiny toy pony.

"Petal! I knew it!" Lindsey burst out crossly. "How mean is that girl? Thank you, Comet."

"You are welcome," Comet neighed, as every last spark faded and the rainbow mist blew away across the grass like glittering dust.

"I'll see you later!" Lindsey said. She had something she had to do.

Chapter
NINE

Lindsey crept back into the cabin and carefully opened the closet. It creaked loudly and she paused, wincing as she looked over her shoulder. Luckily her cabinmates were still asleep.

She quickly finished what she was doing and closed the closet door. Grabbing some clean clothes, she darted into the bathroom and had showered and dressed by the time the other girls were up and about.

"It's no good getting up early to groom that scruffy black-and-white pony. You won't win the prize for most-improved rider!" Tash jeered, pulling on her riding boots.

"That's right. You don't have a chance! Tash always wins that prize," Shawna said.

"Whatever." Lindsey shrugged as she bit back a grin.

"Yeow! What's sticking into me?" Suddenly Tash gave a loud yell as she pulled off her right boot. She tipped it up and a small object fell out.

"Petal! Yay!" Penny cried, snatching up her tiny palomino pony.

"What's that doing in there? It was in my ba— I mean, someone must have put it there," Tash burbled guiltily.

Penny squared her shoulders and
looked Tash in the eye. "I knew you'd
taken her. Don't ever try that again—or
else!"

Tash backed away warily. "But it wasn't
me! I didn't—"

"Don't even," Penny said coldly,

walking away. "Come on, Lins. Let's go and see Chance and Allsorts before breakfast."

Later in the Hay Net there was fresh orange juice and pancakes with maple syrup for a special treat. Afterward, everyone trooped to the tack room for the prizes.

Lindsey breathed in the smells of leather and saddle soap, as she and Penny perched on blanket boxes with the other kids. Lindsey heard a soft neigh and looked around to see Comet's head poking in through an open window.

She smiled at her friend as Gina Morgan began speaking. "The prize isn't just for the most-improved rider. It's also for the rider who's been the best team-player and the most helpful . . ."

Suddenly Lindsey heard a sound she'd

been both hoping for and dreading at the same time.

The hollow sound of galloping hooves overhead.

She froze. *Destiny!* It had to be.

Comet had gone. She heard his eager whinny and knew he was following the magical hoofbeats that were getting louder and closer.

"I'll be right back!" she whispered to Penny, before jumping up and rushing outside.

As she rounded the building, there was a flash and twinkling rainbow mist floated down around Comet. He stood there in his true form. He was no longer a handsome dark brown pony with a white star, but a magnificent cream pony with a noble head and proudly arched neck.

His flowing mane and tail and gold-feathered wings gleamed brightly in the sunshine.

"Comet!" Lindsey gasped. She had almost forgotten how beautiful he was. "Hurry! You have to catch her!" she cried, forcing herself to swallow the lump rising in her throat.

Comet's deep violet eyes softened with affection. "Farewell. You have been a good friend."

"I'll never forget you," she said, her voice breaking. It was hard to let him go, even though she knew this had to happen.

Comet spread his magnificent gold wings. "I will not forget you either. Ride well and true, Lindsey," he said in a deep musical neigh.

Lindsey rushed forward, threw her arms around his silky neck and pressed her face to his glowing warmth for one last time. And then she slowly backed away.

There was a final flash of bright violet light, and a silent burst of rainbow crystals showered down around her and tinkled like tiny bells as they hit the ground.

Comet soared upward. He faded and was gone.

Lindsey stood there, fighting tears. She could hardly believe how fast it had happened. Something glittered on the ground. It was a single shimmering gold wing-feather. As she bent and picked it up, it tingled faintly against her palm and turned to a cream color.

She put it in her pocket, knowing she would always treasure it as a reminder of her wonderful magical friend. After a moment, she took a deep breath and tried very hard not to feel so sad. This was what she had hoped would happen. Comet had found his sister. Now she wouldn't worry about leaving him here all alone.

She walked back to the tack room, just as Penny rushed out to meet her.

"There you are! Gina's looking for you. You won the prize!"

"Really?" Lindsey said in delight, starting to smile in amazement. "I bet Tash's furious."

"She is! Gina's giving her a lecture about being a sore loser!" Penny said triumphantly. "Look, my mom and dad have just arrived. Let's go and tell them our news!"

Lindsey found herself beaming.

Everything had worked out perfectly. "Thank you for everything, Comet. I hope you and Destiny get home safely to Rainbow Mist Island!"

About the
AUTHOR

Sue Bentley's books for children often
include animals, fairies, and wildlife.
She lives in Northampton, England, and
enjoys reading, going to the movies, and
watching the birds on the feeders outside
her window. She loves horses, which she
thinks are all completely magical. One of
her favorite books is *Black Beauty*, which
she must have read at least ten times. At
school she was always getting scolded for
daydreaming, but she now knows that she
was storing up ideas for when she became
a writer. Sue has met and owned many
animals, but the wild creatures in her life
hold a special place in her heart.

Don't miss these Magic Ponies books!

#1 A New Friend

#2 A Special Wish

#3 A Twinkle of Hooves

#4 Show-Jumping Dreams

#5 Winter Wonderland

#6 Riding Rescue

#7 Circus Surprise

Don't miss these Magic Kitten books!

#1 A Summer Spell

#2 Classroom Chaos

#3 Star Dreams

#4 Double Trouble

#5 Moonlight Mischief

#6 A Circus Wish

#7 Sparkling Steps

#8 A Glittering Gallop

#9 Seaside Mystery

A Christmas Surprise

Purrfect Sticker
and Activity Book

Starry Sticker
and Activity Book